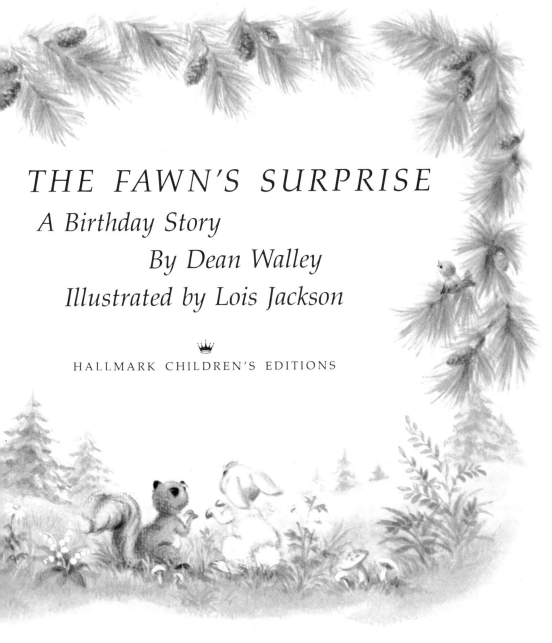

THE FAWN'S SURPRISE

A Birthday Story

By Dean Walley

Illustrated by Lois Jackson

HALLMARK CHILDREN'S EDITIONS

G uess who's having a birthday," said the wise owl. "Not me," said the bunny, "my birthday was last week." "I don't know," said the little raccoon. "But I wish it were mine. I haven't had a birthday in ages!"

The fox, the beaver and the squirrel didn't know who was having a birthday either. So the owl had to tell them. "The fawn is having a birthday. And it's tomorrow!"

"Why don't we give him a party?" said the beaver.

"Yes, a party," said the squirrel.

"A surprise party," said the raccoon.

"With a four-leaf clover cake," said the fox. "I know that's his favorite."

"I'll sing the birthday song," said the bunny, who thought he had a very nice voice.

"We'll all sing the birthday song," said the owl, who was very wise and knew everything about birthdays.

"And we'll give him presents," said the beaver, who knew a little bit about birthdays, too.

So all the animals ran off to find presents and make plans for the fawn's surprise birthday party.

The next day they met by the old hollow tree. They were all ready to have the birthday party.

"But where is the fawn?" asked the beaver.

"Isn't he coming to his own party?" asked the raccoon.

"Don't be silly," said the owl. "The fawn doesn't know he's having a party. It's a surprise. The fox will bring the fawn here without giving away our secret. Then we'll all surprise him!"

The fox was very clever. And he had a plan. He scurried off through the forest to the fawn's home. There he found the fawn sitting by himself and looking very sad.

"What's wrong with you?"asked the fox. "Why aren't you out playing on such a nice day?"

"I feel too sad to play," said the fawn. "Today is my birthday. It's already afternoon, and no one remembered."

"I know how you feel," said the sly fox. "No one ever remembers my birthday either, but I always go to the Birthday Tree and that makes me feel better."

"What's a Birthday Tree anyway?" said the fawn.

"Why, I thought you knew," said the fox. "It's a wonderful tree that grows birthday presents. On your birthday you can pick all you want. Come on! I'll show you!"

The fox ran off and the fawn jumped up and followed him. He was excited just thinking about the Birthday Tree. But when the fox stopped at the old hollow tree, the fawn felt sadder than ever. "This isn't a Birthday Tree!" he cried. "You tricked me!"

But suddenly..."SURPRISE! SURPRISE!" Out from behind the old hollow tree popped the owl and the beaver and the squirrel and the raccoon. They all began to sing:

"Happy Birthday to you,

Happy Birthday to you,

Happy Birthday, dear Fawn,

Happy Birthday to you!"

The fawn was so excited that he sang too. "Oh, a surprise party! This is better than a Birthday Tree!" cried the fawn. "I thought everyone had forgotten me!"

"We didn't forget," said the fox. "We even remembered to get you presents!" And he handed the fawn a piece of honeycomb full of golden honey.

"This looks delicious," said the fawn, who loved honey. "I can eat it just a little at a time on specially happy days."

Then the bunny hopped up with his present, a piece of sparkling rock crystal he had found by the brook.

"What a pretty present," said the fawn. "Whenever I look at it I'll be able to see rainbows."

The beaver had taken a lily pad from the lake and dried it in the sun. The fawn thought it would make a good fan to stir up a breeze with on hot days.

"Here is a pine cone you can use to brush your smooth coat," said the squirrel. "Or you can spin it like a top!"

The raccoon came forward with a hollow reed. He had made little holes in it with his teeth. "It's a flute," said the raccoon. "Just blow on it and you can make music."

Last of all, the wise old owl stepped up with his present. It was a big silver coin he had found in the woods long ago. "You can use this for a mirror," said the owl. "Now you can always be sure you are looking your best."

"These are all wonderful presents," said the fawn. "You can be sure I'll remember all your birthdays, too!"

When it started to get dark, the beaver and the raccoon scampered behind the tree. They came back carrying the four-leaf clover cake. There were fireflies flying around the top of it. They looked even prettier than candles.

"Now it's time to make a wish," said the owl. "Then, if you blow the fireflies away, your wish will come true."

At first, the fawn couldn't decide what to wish.

"Wish for all the berries you can eat," said the fox.

"Why not wish for some carrots?" said the hungry bunny. "You could share them with me."

"No, no! Don't listen to him," said the beaver. "Wish for sunny days and games to play."

"I think you should wish for a secret forest where hunters never go," said the squirrel.

"Wish for more wishes!" cried the raccoon.

"It's your birthday and the wishing is up to you," said the owl. "Just be sure you blow all the fireflies away."

"I know just what to wish," said the fawn. He shut his eyes and whispered to himself, in a voice that only we could hear, "I wish that everyone's birthday will be just as happy as mine has been today."

Then he took a deep breath and blew as hard as he could until all the fireflies flew away into the night.

"What did you wish? What did you wish?" asked the fox and the bunny and the beaver and the squirrel and the raccoon all at the same time.

"You mustn't tell!" cried the owl. "If you tell, your wish won't come true! You have to keep it a secret."

The fawn didn't tell. And his wish came true. It keeps on coming true every day, for birthday animals — and for birthday children, too.